DC
SUPER
HEROES

WONDER WOMAN

AND THE CHEETAH CHALLENGE

WRITTEN BY
LAURIE S. SUTTON

ILLUSTRATED BY
LEONEL CASTELLANI

WONDER WOMAN CREATED BY
WILLIAM MOULTON MARSTON

STONE ARCH BOOKS
a capstone imprint

Published by Stone Arch Books,
an imprint of Capstone.
1710 Roe Crest Drive
North Mankato, Minnesota 56003
www.capstonepub.com

Library of Congress Cataloging–in–Publication Data
Names: Sutton, Laurie, author. | Castellani, Leonel, illustrator.
Title: Wonder Woman and the Cheetah challenge / by Laurie S. Sutton ; illustrated
    by Leonel Castellani
Description: North Mankato, MN : Stone Arch Books, a Capstone imprint, [2020] |
    Series: DC super hero adventures | "Wonder Woman created by William Moulton
    Marston." | Audience: Ages 8–10. | Summary: At the Global Village theme
    park,The Cheetah challenges Wonder Woman to a showdown that ends in the
    Greek showcase.
Identifiers: LCCN 2020001284 (print) | LCCN 2020001285 (ebook) |
    ISBN 9781496597908 (hardcover) | ISBN 9781496599643 (paperback) |
    ISBN 9781496597946 (adobe pdf)
Subjects: CYAC: Supervillains—Fiction. | Superheroes—Fiction. | Amusement
    parks—Fiction.
Classification: LCC PZ7.S968294 Wk 2020 (print) | LCC PZ7.S968294 (ebook) |
    DDC [Fic]—dc23
LC record available at https://lccn.loc.gov/2020001284
LC ebook record available at https://lccn.loc.gov/2020001285

Designer: Brann Garvey

TABLE OF CONTENTS

With countries in chaos and the world at war, Earth faced its darkest hour. To answer its cry for help, the Amazons on the secret island of Themyscira held a trial to find their strongest and bravest champion. From that contest one warrior—Princess Diana—triumphed over all and boldly entered the world of mortals. Now her mission is to conquer villainy, defend justice, and restore peace across the globe.

She is . . .

WONDER WOMAN
™

CHAPTER 1

Running Start

WHOOSH!

Wonder Woman flew at amazing speed through the clear, evening sky. The super hero did not need a plane or rocket to travel this fast. The Amazon warrior was as swift as Hermes, the messenger of the ancient Greek gods—and she did not even need his legendary winged sandals.

Wonder Woman was on her way to the Global Village. It was a theme park made up of exhibits from around the world. She was going to make a speech at the exhibit for the Amazon nation of Themyscira.

When the hero arrived above the Global Village, she looked down at the park. She saw amusement rides and lots of food courts crowded with happy tourists. But the main feature was all the exhibits built to look like small villages or towns.

Wonder Woman could recognize each nation by the style of its buildings. A pagoda decorated with dragons represented China. A Mayan-style pyramid stood in the center of the Central America exhibit.

The hero searched for the building that looked like the famous Greek Parthenon. That was the location of the Amazon exhibit.

Ah, there it is, Wonder Woman thought when she spotted the structure's classic columns. *And it looks like a crowd is already waiting for me.*

Cheering people waved and clapped as Wonder Woman flew down to them. But suddenly another sort of sound reached the Amazon's ears. She heard yelling and shouting coming from somewhere—and it was not the noise of happy tourists. The voices were full of fear.

I hear trouble, Wonder Woman thought. The Amazon warrior stopped in midair and turned in a slow circle. She used her sharp eyesight and hearing to locate the danger.

Uh-oh, something is going on over by the Mayan pyramid, Wonder Woman thought. *I see people running in all directions. I better go check it out.*

Wonder Woman zoomed down toward the exhibit. **WHOOOSH!** It only took a few seconds for her to discover what was causing people to panic.

A woman with the features of a fierce jungle cat stood in the center of a group of security officers. She had a long, feline tail, fangs, and sharp claws on her hands and feet. Her body was covered with tawny yellow fur marked with a pattern of spots.

"The Cheetah!" Wonder Woman said.

The super-villain heard her name and looked up to see Wonder Woman hovering in the air above her.

"Wonder Woman!" The Cheetah snarled. She tightened her grip on a golden jaguar statue in her claws. "I was hoping you'd show up. I've been itching for a good fight!"

"Stop her, Wonder Woman!" a security officer cried. "She stole the statue of Balam from the Mayan exhibit. It's very valuable!"

"You may have superpowers, but you're still a common thief, Cheetah," Wonder Woman declared as she scanned the area. She had to act quickly, but she also needed to protect everyone in the area from harm.

"There's nothing common about me," The Cheetah replied. Before Wonder Woman could react, The Cheetah used the incredible speed of her namesake. She rushed toward the ring of security guards.

Even though the officers held stun-sticks, The Cheetah moved too fast for them to use the weapons. She swiped with her claws and snagged two guards by the fabric of their uniforms. Then she used her tail like a whip to knock the stun-sticks from their grasps.

SMAK! SMAK!

The Cheetah stood with the two officers dangling in the grip of one hand. She held the precious golden statue of Balam in her other hand.

"I have hostages now, Wonder Woman," The Cheetah said. "You and those security guards need to back off. I'm getting out of here with my loot. If you try to stop me, I'll make these two guards pay for your mistake."

I can't allow her to harm those brave officers, Wonder Woman thought as she considered her options. Still hovering in the air, the Amazon turned slowly in a circle to face the rest of the security guards surrounding the super-villain.

"Please back away from The Cheetah," the hero said.

"But . . . Wonder Woman! We can't let her get away with this!" the lead security officer protested.

"A peaceful solution is always better than a violent one," Wonder Woman replied. She continued to turn around in the air. She was using the delay to make sure no tourists were in harm's way. Wonder Woman knew that The Cheetah was not going to give up without a fight.

"Okay . . . ," the lead security officer said. "Everyone, back away from The Cheetah."

The ring of officers stepped backward slowly as Wonder Woman floated in the air above them. The Cheetah watched as the ring widened.

"Clear a path for me to pass," the villain growled. She shook her hostages to show she meant business.

The security officers all looked up at
Wonder Woman to see what they should
do. She nodded, and a section of the ring
opened up.

The sound of police sirens wailed in
the distance. The Cheetah's tail twitched
nervously. More officers were about to arrive
at the park. She knew she had to make her
move—and fast.

ZOOOOM! SWOOOSH!

Suddenly The Cheetah felt the force of a
strong wind. In the next second she felt the
security officers and the golden statue being
snatched out of her hands. At the same time,
she was knocked off-balance and almost
fell to the ground. Her cheetahlike reflexes
saved her, but by the time she recovered she
realized that her hostages were gone. So was
the golden statue of Balam.

Wonder Woman had all of them.

"You're not the only one who can run at amazing speed," Wonder Woman told the super-villain.

The Amazon warrior stood just inside the ring of security officers. She handed the statue to one of the guards she had rescued from The Cheetah's grasp. Then Wonder Woman took the golden Lasso of Truth from her belt and twirled it by her side. She started to walk slowly toward The Cheetah. At the same time, the villain started inching her way backward.

"You have lost the hostages. You have lost your stolen loot. Now you will lose your freedom," Wonder Woman said.

"I won't give up," The Cheetah said with a sneer. "If you want me, you're going to have to catch me."

The super-villain turned swiftly on her catlike feet. Wonder Woman reacted with Amazonian speed and tossed the loop of the golden lasso at The Cheetah.

The super-villain dodged at the last second and then leaped with incredible strength right over the ring of security guards. The feline felon landed in the middle of a nearby crowd of curious tourists and tried to use them as cover to mask her escape.

Like The Cheetah said, if I want her, I'm going to have to catch her, Wonder Woman thought. *Well, I'm up to the challenge!*

CHAPTER 2

Catch Me If You Can!

Wonder Woman took to the air to track The Cheetah. The super-villain was not hard to find. She knocked people over in her rush and left a very clear trail.

If The Cheetah thinks she can use crowds of people in the park to hide her escape, she is very wrong, Wonder Woman thought. *I have to stop her before she hurts someone.*

Wonder Woman swooped down toward the fleeing felon. *WHOOOOSH!* The Amazon warrior reached out to grab The Cheetah like a hunting hawk lunging for its prey.

The super-swift super-villain twisted away and out of the hero's grasp at astounding speed. This made her bump into the people crowding around her. There wasn't very much room to move.

"Hey! Stop shoving!" one tourist said as The Cheetah ran into him.

"How rude!" another person complained.

"Where are your manners?!"

"Ow! Mommy, that mean lady stepped on my foot!"

Suddenly The Cheetah was surrounded by park visitors who were very upset. Everyone turned around and stared at her.

Grrr. My plan to escape by hiding in a crowd is actually working against me, The Cheetah thought. Desperate, the super-villain looked for an easier way out.

RUUUMBLE! ZWOOOSH! WHEEE!

The sounds of something moving quickly attracted The Cheetah's attention. She bared her sharp fangs and smiled when she saw what it was.

A roller coaster! The Cheetah thought. *That should help me make a quick escape.*

"Not so fast, Cheetah," Wonder Woman said as she landed in front of the villain. The crowd of tourists cleared a space around the Amazon warrior and the feline felon.

"Ha! 'Fast' is my middle name," The Cheetah said as she rushed toward Wonder Woman with her sharp claws.

The Amazon held up her metal bracelets to defend herself against the super-villain's attack. But The Cheetah's blow did not come. Instead, the feline felon used her forward speed to launch herself over Wonder Woman. She landed on the roof of a ticket booth next to the nearby roller coaster.

"Actually, I don't really have a middle name," The Cheetah said, laughing as she paused on the roof.

"Maybe not. But if you did, it would be 'Running Out of Breath,'" Wonder Woman said. "I can hear you getting tired."

"*Grrr!*" The Cheetah growled. She *was* getting tired. Like her animal namesake, her speed came in bursts. It did not last for long.

Wonder Woman knew the super-villain's weakness. The Amazon could chase The Cheetah until the villain was exhausted.

But Wonder Woman also knew her strategy might come at a price. The Cheetah, like a wild animal, would be even more dangerous if she were cornered or thought she had nothing to lose.

"Give up, Cheetah. Please," the Amazon warrior said. "Don't harm yourself trying to escape."

"Like you said before . . . I've lost my loot and my hostages," The Cheetah replied. "I have nothing left except my freedom. And I will not lose that."

RUUUUMBLE! RUUUMBLE! SQUEEEEAL!

A train of roller coaster cars sped on a stretch of tracks near the ticket booth. Without so much as a glance, the feline felon launched herself into the air toward the speeding roller coaster cars.

Wonder Woman moved at the same time the super-villain did. The Amazon warrior whipped the Lasso of Truth at The Cheetah. The lasso missed its mark by an inch. The Cheetah did not. The villain grabbed onto one of the passing roller coaster cars.

"Argh!" The Cheetah groaned as her tired arm and shoulder muscles strained to hold onto the speeding car.

Wonder Woman watched as the villain almost lost her grip.

She's going to fall, Wonder Woman worried. *She may be my enemy, but I can't just stand by and let her hurt herself.*

Wonder Woman leaped into the air. She flew toward the speeding roller coaster cars. Her Amazon abilities allowed her to keep just ahead of the cars as they roared along the twisting tracks.

The roller coaster riders cheered and shouted at the sight of the hero. What fun! What a bonus! But they had no idea a dangerous villain was hitching a ride at the back of the train.

The roller coaster cars reached the base of a steep hill and started to zoom upward. Wonder Woman landed atop one of the front cars and started to walk back toward The Cheetah.

"Please keep your hands inside the cars," Wonder Woman said as the riders waved their arms in the air, excited for the big drop they knew was coming next.

Wonder Woman knew it was coming too. She was counting on the moment of almost zero gravity as the roller coaster train paused at the peak of the track.

WHOOOOSH!

The roller coaster raced downward. **WHEEEE!** the riders screamed with delight.

Wonder Woman jumped a few feet into the air. The roller coaster cars sped on without her. She hovered in the air for a few seconds and watched the car carrying The Cheetah race toward her.

THWUMP! Wonder Woman dropped down out of the air and landed next to The Cheetah. The Amazon used her incredible speed to grab the super-villain by the wrist.

"Got you! Give up, Cheetah," Wonder Woman said.

"*Rrreeoow!*" The Cheetah snarled.

The super-villain was not ready to surrender. She jumped up and slashed at Wonder Woman with the claws on both of her feet.

At the same moment The Cheetah attacked, the roller coaster went into a giant loop. Suddenly Wonder Woman and her foe were upside down. But only Wonder Woman's feet remained firmly on the cars.

The Cheetah almost flew out of Wonder Woman's grip. But the Amazon warrior's super-strength kept her foe from falling to the ground far below. Even so, The Cheetah's will to escape was strong. She struggled against Wonder Woman's life-saving hold.

"It's time to get back on the ground," Wonder Woman said.

Still holding onto The Cheetah, Wonder Woman jumped off the roller coaster. She used its extreme speed to launch them like a slingshot across the theme park.

CHAPTER 3

Fast Food

As Wonder Woman and The Cheetah sailed over the Global Village theme park, the hero held on tight to keep her foe safe. But the ungrateful villain slashed and struggled the whole time. Wonder Woman could barely control their direction. Still, the Amazon warrior managed to land on her feet in the middle of an outdoor food court.

THWUUUMP!

The impact sent small shock waves through the pavement. It shook the colorful tables and chairs surrounding the food stand and knocked over a few of the patio umbrellas. The people eating in the courtyard jumped to their feet in surprise.

The hard landing jarred The Cheetah loose from Wonder Woman's grasp. The feline felon squirmed free of the Amazon warrior's grip.

"*Hisss!* If you think I'm grateful that you saved me, you're wrong," The Cheetah said.

"I don't expect gratitude or thanks," Wonder Woman said with a shrug. "You were in danger, and I acted. It was the right thing to do."

"Ugh. Heroes," The Cheetah sneered. Then she leaped toward her enemy with her fangs and claws.

Wonder Woman met The Cheetah's slashing attack with her Amazon bracelets. **SHHIING! ZIIING!** The Cheetah's claws slid across the metal but did not make a mark.

"Don't you know by now that nothing can harm my bracelets?" Wonder Woman told her foe. "They were made by the Greek god Hephaestus."

"Ha. He sounds like the Greek god of sneezes," The Cheetah said with a laugh, but her laugh hid her worry. She needed to stall Wonder Woman a little longer to regain her speed.

The Cheetah looked around for something she could use as a weapon against her enemy. Her speed might be weakening, but she still had most of her strength left. She grabbed an empty chair and threw it at Wonder Woman.

BLAAANG!

Wonder Woman knocked it aside with one of her bracelets. The Cheetah swiftly picked up another chair and tossed it.

KLAAANG!

The chair bounced off the other bracelet. Both chairs flew through the air and landed in a nearby fountain with a huge splash.

"Everyone, please clear the area while I take care of this menace," Wonder Woman told the tourists.

The people scrambled away from the battleground, but they did not go far. They wanted to watch this epic fight. The Cheetah saw this and knew she could use it to her advantage. She knew that Wonder Woman would never let innocent people be harmed, so she decided to use them as a distraction.

If Wonder Woman is busy protecting all those annoying tourists, she won't be chasing me, The Cheetah thought. *Which will give me time to rest and regain my speed.*

The Cheetah picked up a heavy table and threw it at the crowd.

"No!" Wonder Woman shouted.

The Amazon warrior raced to catch the table. She succeeded, but the table was full of food, and all of it hit Wonder Woman.

SPLOOSH! SPLAAAT!

Suddenly Wonder Woman was covered in hot dogs, hamburgers, and relish. The crowd gasped in surprise.

"Ha! Ha! Ha!" The Cheetah laughed at the sight of food dripping off the super hero. It also gave her an idea about how to humiliate her enemy.

The Cheetah ran over to the food service area. She grabbed an armload of small pies, cupcakes, and other desserts from one of the display cases. Then the villain started throwing them at Wonder Woman as fast as she could.

At least she stopped throwing tables and chairs, Wonder Woman thought as she used her bracelets to block the flying food. *Cupcakes and donuts won't hurt anyone.*

The Amazon warrior slowly advanced toward The Cheetah. As she passed a table loaded with a family's abandoned dinner, Wonder Woman suddenly smiled. She picked up several cheese-filled tacos with one hand and a bunch of fish sticks with the other.

"You sure can dish it out, Cheetah, but can you take it?" Wonder Woman said with a sly grin.

ZIIIP! ZIIIP!

With a flick of her wrist, the flaky fish sticks flew toward The Cheetah like mini missiles.

ZIIING! ZIIING!

The cheesy tacos followed. The feline felon dodged the gooey onslaught, but a big blob of cheese sauce landed on her cheek.

"*Grrr!*" The Cheetah growled.

"I don't think we're even," Wonder Woman said as she lifted another tray of food from a nearby table. The Amazon warrior was still dripping with mustard and relish from the villain's first attack.

Wonder Woman used her pinpoint accuracy to hurl a hailstorm of chicken nuggets at The Cheetah.

BOP! BOP! BOP!

The flying finger food pelted the villain. Wonder Woman followed up with handfuls of macaroni and cheese. *SPLAT! SPLOOSH!* The Cheetah could not match the Amazon warrior's speed.

"I think you need some fruit in your diet," Wonder Woman said as she pitched a half dozen apples and oranges at The Cheetah like baseballs.

The super-villain used her sharp claws to slice through most of the fruit before it reached her.

I better get out of here before Wonder Woman throws the whole food pyramid at me, The Cheetah thought.

The super-villain turned tail and fled inside the food service building. Wonder Woman quickly chased her into the kitchen.

The Cheetah soon realized her mistake. There was very little room to move around in there. She was trapped!

Wonder Woman faced the feline villain. She watched The Cheetah's desperation grow. The villain flattened her back against the stainless steel refrigerator and raked her claws on the metal. **SKREEEECH!** The Cheetah was trapped, and she knew it.

This is what I was worried about, Wonder Woman thought. *Now she's more dangerous than ever.*

CHAPTER 4

Fighting Dirty

Wonder Woman knew she had to move fast to capture The Cheetah at last. The feline felon looked as if she was about to take desperate action. The Amazon raced forward at amazing speed and grabbed The Cheetah by both wrists.

The two opponents were suddenly up close and face-to-face. Both of them were covered in food.

Mustard dripped off Wonder Woman's chin. Cupcake icing clung to her hair and apple pie filling hung from her uniform. Blobs of cheesy macaroni and chicken nuggets stuck to The Cheetah's fur.

"*Sniff, sniff.* You stink," The Cheetah said and wrinkled her nose.

"Are you sure what you're smelling is coming from *me*?" Wonder Woman replied. "You should take a look at yourself."

"And I'll make you pay for that," The Cheetah promised. "A cat likes to stay clean."

"You started it," Wonder Woman reminded the villain.

It took a few moments for Wonder Woman to realize that The Cheetah was not fighting back. She wasn't desperately trying to escape.

Has the super-villain finally had enough?
Wonder Woman thought.

"I'm glad to see you've finally decided to surrender peacefully, Cheetah," Wonder Woman said as she reached for her Lasso of Truth with one hand.

But by now The Cheetah was feeling her speed return. She'd had time to rest. It wasn't much, but it was just enough. Wonder Woman had only one hand on The Cheetah. The villain took advantage of that.

"*Reeeow!*" The Cheetah snarled as she twisted and slashed at the hero.

Wonder Woman tightened her grip on the villain's wrist and pulled sideways with her Amazon strength. The Cheetah was stopped in mid-motion. Then Wonder Woman whipped out with one leg and knocked her foe's feet out from under her.

WHOMMMP!

The Cheetah landed face-first on the kitchen floor.

"*Ooof!*" the villain gasped as the breath was knocked out of her.

"I knew you were up to something," Wonder Woman said as she put her knee on the middle of the villain's back to hold her down. She pulled The Cheetah's hands behind her back and then reached for the golden lasso to tie up the villain at last.

Suddenly The Cheetah's tail whipped out at Wonder Woman.

SMAAAK! It hit Wonder Woman across her face. **SPLAAAT!** The mustard, relish, and other foods still clinging to the Amazon splashed into her eyes.

"*Ahhh!*" Wonder Woman gasped.

The Cheetah used this brief distraction to break free of the hero. The villain jumped to her feet. She grabbed the first thing she could find to use as a weapon against her foe. When Wonder Woman wiped the icing and mustard from her eyes, she saw The Cheetah standing ready to battle with . . .

"A spatula?" Wonder Woman said in surprise. "You're going to fight me with a kitchen tool?"

The Cheetah quickly grabbed a large metal mixing bowl and lifted it in front of her like a shield.

"Well, I have fought warriors wielding stranger weapons," Wonder Woman said with a shrug.

The Amazon warrior leaped feet first at the mixing bowl that The Cheetah held up as a shield.

KRUUUUMP!

The thin metal crumpled as if it were made of aluminum foil. The force of the blow threw The Cheetah backward.

SLAAAM!

She hit a wall of storage shelves. Containers filled with vegetables and chopped lettuce fell on the villain as she slowly collapsed to the floor.

A head of broccoli rolled up against Wonder Woman's foot. The Amazon warrior used the tip of her boot to flip it up into her hand.

"Now, come quietly and I won't make you eat your vegetables," Wonder Woman said as she tossed the broccoli up and down.

"I'm not going to do either of those things," The Cheetah said.

The Cheetah threw the spatula at Wonder Woman. The object was not dangerous, but she knew the super hero would deflect it with her bracelets. Sure enough, Wonder Woman did just that. *PLIIING!*

The Cheetah used those few seconds to scramble toward something else that she could use as a defense. The super-villain snatched the spray hose hanging above the kitchen sink and pointed it at Wonder Woman.

"Another unusual weapon of choice. But I believe broccoli is better," the hero said.

The Amazon warrior threw the head of broccoli with the speed of a cannonball. The Cheetah dodged the broccoli with her renewed speed.

"Missed," The Cheetah said with a sneer. "My turn."

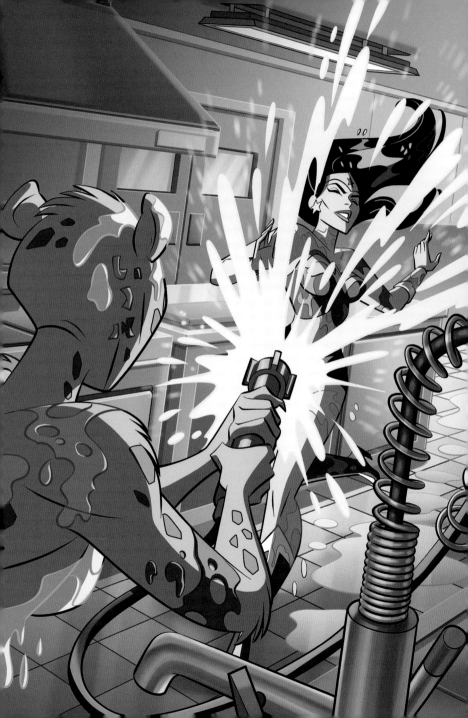

The Cheetah used the dishwashing sprayer to drench Wonder Woman with a powerful jet of water. The Amazon stepped backward and held up her arms for protection. The villain laughed. When she finally finished, she howled at the sight of the soaked super hero standing in a puddle of water.

"Ha! Ha! Ha! You look worse than a wet cat!" The Cheetah laughed at her foe.

Wonder Woman shook the water from her head, arms, and legs.

"Actually, I must thank you," Wonder Woman replied. "You just washed off all the food. No more mustard in my eyes."

The Cheetah realized that she had accidentally given her foe the advantage. She dropped the sprayer and dashed out of the kitchen the way she had come in.

Wonder Woman followed The Cheetah back out into the food courtyard, but the villain had disappeared.

"She jumped up onto the roof!" one of the tourists shouted helpfully.

"She went that way!" another person said.

Everyone pointed in the same direction.

"Thank you," Wonder Woman replied and launched into the air.

WHOOSH!

Looking out over the theme park, Wonder Woman could see The Cheetah fleeing across the tops of the nearby buildings. She could also see that the theme park security teams and the local police had a couple of helicopters in the air. They were buzzing around the super-villain.

If those helicopters get too close to The Cheetah, there's no telling what she'll do, Wonder Woman thought. *This situation is getting too dangerous for too many people. I have to get her away from everyone.*

In the distance, the Greek Parthenon loomed. It was the home of the Amazon exhibit.

Hmmm. If I could get The Cheetah to go inside the Amazon exhibit, I would be in familiar territory and she would not, Wonder Woman thought. *I would have the advantage.*

But the Amazon warrior knew she was going to need a little help to make her plan work. She zoomed toward one of the helicopters.

CHAPTER 5

Battle of the Titans

Wonder Woman flew up to the police helicopter. She slid open the back hatch door and shouted instructions to the pilot.

"I need you and the other helicopter to help me herd The Cheetah toward the Greek Parthenon," Wonder Woman said.

"Okay. I'll radio the other pilot," the officer said. He didn't know why Wonder Woman was making this odd request, but he was willing to help.

Wonder Woman jumped away from the helicopter and swooped toward The Cheetah. The police copter banked and dived toward the super-villain. So did the park security helicopter.

Wonder Woman and the helicopters surrounded The Cheetah on three sides. She had nowhere to go except in the direction Wonder Woman wanted.

The Parthenon was the only place The Cheetah saw as an escape. As soon as she ran inside, she realized it was not as safe as she had thought. The villain found herself in the middle of an epic battle!

Giant warriors towered over her. They fought with swords and spears and were dressed in armor that looked like it was from ancient Greek history.

ZWOOOSH!

A huge sword came straight at The Cheetah. She used her amazing speed to duck under the blade. Then a giant spear whipped past her.

ZIIIP!

The Cheetah spun around to avoid the blow and came face-to-face with a huge muscle-bound man with one eye in the middle of his forehead.

"A Cyclops!" The Cheetah gasped. "What's going on here? Where am I?"

The villain did not have time to find out. *RUMBLE! RUMBLE! RUMBLE!* The ground shook and a tremendous crack in the earth opened up at her feet. The force threw The Cheetah to the ground. A moment later a gigantic dog with three heads leaped up out of the opening. His ferocious bark was almost ear-shattering.

"Th-that's Cerberus, the hound of Hades," The Cheetah said. "First Cyclops and now this monster?"

Suddenly a man in black armor leaped out of the crack. A horde of deathly pale bodies followed him.

"Oh no! That's Hades," The Cheetah said. "These are people from Greek myth. This can't be real."

KRACK-A-BOOOOM!

A bolt of lightning struck between The Cheetah and the Cyclops. The one-eyed giant was thrown backward. Cerberus snatched Cyclops up in one of his three jaws and shook him like a chew toy.

The Cheetah looked up from where she lay on the ground. She quickly spotted where the lightning bolt had come from.

A man in golden robes towered taller than all the other people. He held white-hot bolts of lightning in his hands like a bunch of spears.

"Zeus!" The Cheetah gasped. "He's the Greek god of Olympus. Now I know this can't be real."

"You have traveled though time to the Battle of the Titans against the Gods of Olympus," a woman's voice said. The Cheetah turned and saw a beautiful goddess in shimmering robes. The goddess reached out to the fallen super-villain. "Give me your hand and I will take you to safety."

"Who are you?" The Cheetah asked. All the sights and sounds were overwhelming. She could hardly think straight. But the goddess was calm in the center of the confusion.

"I am Artemis, goddess of the hunt," the woman replied. "I protect all animals."

"Okay, I could use a little help," The Cheetah said as she held out her hand to be pulled to her feet.

Suddenly the goddess clamped down on The Cheetah's wrist with a grip like iron.

CLAMP!

Surprised, the villain tried to pull away. But there was no escape.

A moment later, Wonder Woman stepped through the image of Artemis. That was when The Cheetah realized it was Wonder Woman holding onto her wrist and not the goddess Artemis.

"I *knew* none of this could be real. This is all a big fake!" The Cheetah hissed as she tried to twist free.

Suddenly the Greek god of the sea, Poseidon, ran forward. He threw his golden trident toward Wonder Woman and her captive.

WHOOSH!

The Cheetah gasped, but the Amazon warrior did not flinch. The weapon simply passed through them without harm.

"Actually it's a hologram," Wonder Woman said. "It's part of the Greek exhibit to teach people about the nation's rich cultural history."

"*Grrr!*" The Cheetah growled as she tried to twist out of Wonder Woman's grip.

The Amazon warrior held on tight as the villain rolled sideways. She swiped at Wonder Woman with the claws on her feet, but the Amazon jumped over them just in time.

In the few seconds that Wonder Woman's feet were in the air, The Cheetah pulled against the Amazon's grip. Wonder Woman did not let go, but without her feet firmly braced on the ground, she was easily pulled off-balance.

WHAM!

The hero fell on top of The Cheetah. Wonder Woman quickly wrapped her arms and legs around the super-villain in a wrestling hold.

"Did you know that wrestling was invented by the Greeks?" Wonder Woman said as she pinned her opponent to the ground.

"I have a few moves of my own," The Cheetah said as she slashed at Wonder Woman with her tail.

"That's against the rules," Wonder Woman said.

"I never follow the rules," The Cheetah declared.

The two combatants rolled across the holographic battlefield, still locked together in a full-body clutch. They tumbled out of the historic display and into another one.

CRASH!

When they stopped, The Cheetah looked up. She was surprised to see that she was surrounded by fierce female warriors.

"Meet the Amazons of Themyscira," Wonder Woman told the super-villain.

The Cheetah's surprise did not last for long. The warriors held their weapons as if in the middle of a battle, but none of them moved.

"They're statues! Another fake," The Cheetah said. Then she looked closer at the weapons. "But those swords aren't fake. Actually, they look valuable. They could make up for my losing that jaguar statue."

The Cheetah realized she had one last chance to escape with some loot. Using a burst of strength, the super-villain broke free from Wonder Woman. She leaped like a cat toward the nearest statue and grabbed its sword. The weapon did not come loose.

"No!" The Cheetah growled. She raced from statue to statue. All of the swords were firmly attached. "This whole heist is a bust. I'm getting out of here."

The feline felon jumped on top of one of the statues. She stood upright and balanced like a cat on a fence as she looked for the exit from the exhibit.

Suddenly the loop of Wonder Woman's golden lasso dropped over her.

SHNUUUG!

The lasso tightened around the villain.

"Surrender, Cheetah," Wonder Woman said. The Cheetah did not resist. The power of the Lasso of Truth made the villain obey.

Moments later, Wonder Woman walked out of the Greek exhibit with the captured super-villain. Tourists cheered. Police and park security officers rushed forward to take The Cheetah to jail. Wonder Woman raised a hand to stop them.

"Wait. The Cheetah must make up for all the damage she has caused," Wonder Woman said.

Wonder Woman squeezed the Lasso of Truth. It glowed around The Cheetah.

"Cheetah, I command you to clean up the mess you made," Wonder Woman said.

A park caretaker tossed a broom toward the super-villain.

"*Grrr!*" The Cheetah growled as she caught it with her catlike reflexes. Still bound by the Lasso of Truth, she got to work.

The Cheetah

REAL NAME: Barbara Ann Minerva

SPECIES: Mutated Human

OCCUPATION: Biologist

HEIGHT: 5 feet 9 inches

WEIGHT: 120 pounds

EYES: Green

HAIR: Auburn

POWERS/ABILITIES: Superhuman strength, speed, and agility. Her claws and teeth are razor sharp, capable of slicing through stone.

BIOGRAPHY: The Cheetah was once an accomplished scientist named Barbara Ann Minerva. She was tireless in her efforts to enhance humans with animal abilities. When funding for her project was cut off, Minerva experimented on herself. The results were terrifying. She'd become a hybrid creature that was half-human, half-cheetah. Though she now possessed increased strength and the enhanced abilities of the cheetah, her mind was fractured. She'd developed a villainous streak that led her to commit crimes. Though she's fallen in with a variety of criminal organizations, deep within The Cheetah there's still a part of her that hopes to one day become normal again.

- The Cheetah doesn't always work alone. She once joined forces with Lex Luthor as a member of his Injustice Gang. The villainess has also worked with Gorilla Grodd in his Legion of Doom.

- The Cheetah is Wonder Woman's most cunning and clever enemy. Her catlike agility and super-strength make her a formidable fighter too. To make matters worse, The Cheetah is prone to animal-like rages at any given moment.

- The Cheetah can put up a good fight, but she's no match for Wonder Woman's Lasso of Truth. The golden rope can ensnare the villainess, weakening her super-speed and super-strength. More importantly, the lasso always gets to the root of The Cheetah's trickery by forcing her to speak nothing but the truth.

BIOGRAPHIES

Author

Laurie S. Sutton has been reading comics since she was a kid. She grew up to become an editor for Marvel, DC Comics, Starblaze, and Tekno Comics. She has written *Adam Strange* for DC, *Star Trek: Voyager* for Marvel, plus *Star Trek: Deep Space Nine* and *Witch Hunter* for Malibu Comics. There are long boxes of comics in her closet where there should be clothing and shoes. Laurie has lived all over the world and currently resides in Florida.

Illustrator

Leonel Castellani has worked as a comic artist and illustrator for more than twenty years. Mostly known for his work on licensed art for companies such as Warner Bros., DC Comics, Disney, Marvel Entertainment, and Cartoon Network, Leonel has also built a career as a conceptual designer and storyboard artist for video games, movies, and TV. In addition to drawing, Leonel also likes to sculpt and paint. He currently lives in La Plata City, Argentina.

GLOSSARY

desperation (dess-puh-RAY-shuhn)—a willingness to do anything to change a situation

exhibit (ig-ZI-buht)—a display that usually includes objects and information to show and tell people about a certain subject

feline (FEE-line)—any animal of the cat family

felon (FEL-uhn)—a criminal convicted of severe crimes, such as armed robbery

gratitude (GRAT-uh-tood)—a feeling of being grateful and thankful

hologram (HOL-uh-gram)—an image made by laser beams that looks three-dimensional

hostage (HOSS-tij)—a person held against his or her will

humiliate (hyoo-MIL-ee-ate)—to make someone look or feel foolish or embarrassed

menace (MEN-iss)—a threat or danger

namesake (NAYM-sayk)—someone or something that a person or thing is named after

surrender (suh-REN-dur)—to give up or admit defeat

DISCUSSION QUESTIONS

1. While battling The Cheetah, Wonder Woman must also protect everyone else at the Global Village theme park from harm. How does keeping others safe make it more difficult for the hero to capture the super-villain?

2. Wonder Woman and The Cheetah fight each other on a roller coaster, in a food court, and in a holographic Greek exhibit. Which setting did you like the best and why?

3. At the end of the story, The Cheetah is forced to clean up the mess she made in the park. Why does Wonder Woman make her do this? Why doesn't she just send the villain to prison right away?

WRITING PROMPTS

1. When Wonder Woman arrives at the theme park, The Cheetah has already stolen the statue of Balam. But how did the super-villain do it? Write a prologue to this story that shows the villain sneaking into the Mayan exhibit and stealing the statue.

2. The Cheetah uses her catlike animal powers to battle Wonder Woman. If you could have the powers of any animal, which would you choose? Write a short paragraph describing your powers and draw a picture of what you would look like.

3. What happens to The Cheetah after she cleans up the theme park? Does she go to prison or does she somehow escape? Write another chapter that describes the continuing adventures of the feline super-villain.

LOOK FOR MORE
DC SUPER HERO ADVENTURES